20°   0°   20°

LONDON

QUEENSTOWN
SOUTHAMPTON

by STEVE BREZENOFF

RETURN TO
TITANIC

AN UNSINKABLE SHIP

3

ILLUSTRATED by SCOTT MURPHY

STONE ARCH BOOKS A CAPSTONE IMPRINT

★ WHITE STAR LINE

SHIP **R.M.S. TITANIC** WEIGHT **46,000** [TONS]

DAY 11 MONTH APRIL YEAR 2012

	NAME	AGE
1	TUCKER PAULSON	14
2	MAYA CHO	14
3		
4		
5		
6		
7		
8		

Published by Stone Arch Books – A Capstone Imprint • 1710 Roe Crest Drive, North Mankato, Minnesota 56003
www.capstonepub.com

Library of Congress Cataloging-in-Publication Data is available on the Library of Congress website.
Library binding: 978-1-4342-3301-1 • Paperback: 978-1-4342-3911-2

Summary: Tucker and Maya join the *Titanic* survivors in the lifeboats as they wait and hope for rescue.

Image Credits: Alamy: Mary Evans Picture Library, 110 (left); AP Images: Stanley Leary, 110 (bottom right); Library of Congress: Chronicling America, Library of Virginia, Richmond, VA, 110 (top right)

Editor: Alison Deering
Designer and Art Director: Bob Lentz
Creative Director: Heather Kindseth

Printed in the United States of America in Stevens Point, Wisconsin.
102011   006404WZS12

CONTENTS

NEW YORK

GREENVILLE

LOCKED UP

Maya and Tucker were in big trouble. They sat at a long conference table in a meeting room at the Greenville History Museum. They were being punished for what had happened the day before.

It's not like they'd been able to help time traveling back to 1912, though. Well, technically that wasn't true. The first time they'd gone back to the *Titanic* had been an accident. Yesterday they'd used a teacup from the Special Collection to go back on purpose. Once their new friend Liam and his parents boarded the *Titanic* as third-class passengers, they couldn't just abandon him on the doomed ship.

But the teacup they'd used had broken when they came back to the present. Even though the teacup in the exhibit was fine, Tucker's mother had been furious. And since they couldn't exactly tell her the truth — especially when they didn't fully understand it themselves — they were stuck in this room.

A low humming sound filled the room. It sounded like a refrigerator, or maybe an air conditioner. But since there was nothing in the room besides them and their homework, Tucker didn't know what it was.

"Ugh," Maya finally said. "What is that noise?" She slammed her pencil down in her open textbook.

"I don't know," Tucker said. "Just ignore it." He didn't look up from his science book.

"I can't ignore it. It's driving me crazy," Maya said. She picked up her pencil and twirled it like a tiny baton. Then she started tapping it on the edge of the conference table.

Tucker did his best to ignore her. He knew it was his fault they were stuck in there to begin with. After all, this was his mom's museum. And using the teacup to go back to the *Titanic* yesterday had been his idea. He was the reason they were spending their spring break stuck in a conference room.

Why did he care what happened to that boy Liam, anyway?

"This is all your fault!" Maya snapped.

Tucker sighed and nodded slightly. "I know," he said under his breath.

"Don't even try to deny it!" Maya said. She spun in her chair to face him and pointed her pencil at him accusingly.

"I won't," Tucker said.

"Do you know how much trouble I got in last night?" Maya asked. "My parents were furious that we broke part of the *Titanic* exhibit. They said they thought it would be impossible for even *me* to get into trouble at a museum on spring break."

"I'm sorry," Tucker said. "I really am."

Maya sighed. "It's my fault, too, I guess," she admitted. "You didn't exactly force me to go back. I could have said no." Maya flopped back into her chair. She put her elbows on the table and dropped her head into her hands. "I can't take this. I'm going to die of boredom. We have to get out of here."

"We can't," Tucker said. "My mom told us not to leave this room. Plus, the door's locked."

"Quitter," Maya said. She sat up straight and looked around the conference room. It was sparsely decorated. There was the table they were using, and the eight chairs around it. In one corner there was an easel with a giant pad of white paper on it, along with a thick black marker.

There were no windows. The walls were nearly bare. One framed poster of George Washington crossing the Delaware hung across from Maya. Near the floor directly under the poster was a big vent. Maya stood up and went over to it.

"I bet this is where that noise is coming from," she said. She bent down to put her ear to it. "Yup. It definitely is."

Tucker sighed. "Maya, I'm sorry we're stuck in here," he said. "I really am. But I just want to get my homework done. I mean, we might as well, right? There's nothing else to do."

Maya didn't respond. She was too busy peering through the wall vent. "I can see another room through here," she said.

"That's terrific," Tucker said, rolling his eyes. "Now will you please be quiet so I can finish reading?" He turned back to his book and tried to keep his mind on his science homework.

"I'm serious, Tucker," Maya said. "I think it's the storeroom."

Tucker looked up from his book. He thought about the path his mom had led them on yesterday. It was a pretty long walk from the storeroom to the conference room. There was no way the storeroom was next door.

It can't be, Tucker thought. He dug through his book bag and pulled out a frayed brochure.

"What's that?" Maya asked. She leaned across the conference table to see.

"A map of the museum," Tucker said, opening the brochure. He pointed to the conference room on the map. "We're here. The storeroom —" he pointed to one of the biggest rooms on the map "— is here."

Tucker traced his finger along the hallway, showing Maya the long walk between the door to the storeroom and the door to the conference room. "See?" he said. "Not even close."

"But they share this wall," Maya said. She stabbed the map with her finger. "Yeah, it takes a long time to walk from one to the other. But it wouldn't take long if there was a door right there."

"Well, there isn't," Tucker said. He folded up the map and put it away. "End of story."

"But there's a vent," Maya said. "Which is basically a door."

"Basically?" Tucker repeated. "Maya, I hate to break it to you, but a vent and a door are not 'basically' the same thing."

Maya ignored him. She grabbed her messenger bag off the floor and dropped it onto the conference room table. Then she opened the bag and dug around inside. "Here it is," she said after a moment. She proudly held up a pink multi-tool.

"Why do you have that in your bag?" Tucker asked.

Maya shrugged. "Just in case," she said. "That's what my dad says." She walked over to the wall and knelt down next to the vent. Using the screwdriver on the multi-tool, she started unscrewing the cover.

"Hey!" Tucker said. He jumped up, ran over to Maya, and snatched away the tool. "Are you nuts?"

"Not yet," Maya said, "but if I have to stay in here much longer, I might go totally insane. Give me that!"

"No way," Tucker said. "We're in enough trouble already." He held the tool behind his back. Maya grabbed for it, but Tucker dodged and ducked.

Maya stopped. She smiled. "You're right, we are in trouble," she said. "And you know who's in even more trouble?"

Tucker squinted at her. "Who?" he asked.

"Liam," Maya said. "Who is stuck back in 1912, on a big old boat that just hit an iceberg."

Tucker's shoulders dropped.

"But," Maya continued, "if you give me that screwdriver, I'll pop this vent cover off, and we can crawl through to the storeroom. Your mom will never know."

"Why do you suddenly care so much about saving Liam?" Tucker asked.

"Oh, please," Maya said. "I just want to get out of here. Another adventure on the *Titanic* is as good an excuse as anything else."

Tucker crossed his arms. "That's it?" he asked.

Maya shrugged. "Well, and Liam is an okay kid," she admitted. "We should help him."

Tucker weighed the two options in his mind. He really didn't want to get in trouble again, but he couldn't stop thinking about the Kearneys. He couldn't just leave them. Tucker sighed.

"Fine," he said. He handed Maya her tool back. "But we have to be quick. And quiet."

"No problem!" Maya said. And she got to work on the screws.

NEW YORK

GREENVILLE

★ WHITE STAR LINE
04.11.2012

THE SPECIAL COLLECTION

Getting the vent cover off in the conference room was easy. But removing the vent on the storeroom side was harder than they'd expected. Maya had to reach through the grate to loosen the screws. Eventually, though, she got it off. It hit the concrete floor of the storeroom with a loud *clang*!

"Shh!" Tucker whispered frantically. "My mom and the security guard will be here in no time if you keep making so much noise."

"Relax," Maya said. "It wasn't that loud." She crawled through the vent and into the storeroom. "Come on. And grab my bag, okay?"

Tucker picked up Maya's bag from the table. Then he ducked and crawled through the vent.

"I can't believe we're doing this," he muttered.

Maya laughed and shook her head. "You're hilarious," she said.

"What do you mean?" Tucker asked. "I wasn't trying to be funny."

"We've gone back in time," Maya said. "*Twice*. And you're worrying about sneaking around in your mom's museum? Doesn't really seem like a big deal at this point. The laws of time and space have already been broken. Does it really matter if we break one tiny little rule at the museum?"

"Good point," Tucker said. He glanced around the storeroom. "Where's that Special Collection?"

Maya pointed across the room, and together they walked over to the magical crate.

"Only two things left," Tucker said. "That broken violin and the life vest."

Maya pulled the life vest out of the crate. It was in a sealed plastic bag.

"Good thinking," Tucker said. "Let's try the life vest. It will probably bring us back to when they're loading the lifeboats."

"Uh-uh," Maya said, shaking her head. "No way. Let's try the violin."

"What does the violin have to do with anything?" Tucker asked. He grabbed the plastic bag with the life vest in it and opened it. The sour, musty scent of mildew immediately filled the air.

Maya covered her nose. "Oh, gross, it stinks!" she said. "That's why I want to try the violin. The life vest is disgusting! I am not touching it."

Tucker couldn't argue with that. The life vest really stunk. He dropped the bag and covered his nose. "Okay, fair enough," he said. "We can try the violin first."

Together, they reached into the crate and pulled out the plastic case that held the violin. It was very fragile looking. Most of the strings were snapped, and the neck was broken in half. The wood looked like it would splinter into a million pieces at the slightest touch.

"Let's be careful about the case this time," Tucker said. I don't need a repeat of the teacup incident with my mom."

Maya held up her multi-tool. "Leave it to me," she said. After a few minutes, the case was open.

"Ready?" Tucker asked.

Maya nodded and held out her hand. Tucker grabbed it and took a deep breath. "On the count of three," he said. "One, two, three!" Together they grabbed the violin and disappeared.

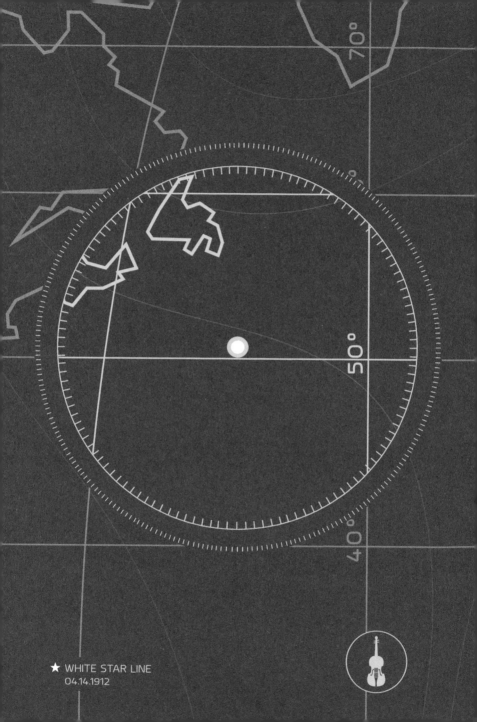

70°

50°

40°

★ WHITE STAR LINE
04.14.1912

3

A MINOR INCIDENT

"Ow," Tucker groaned. Like the first two times they'd made the jump back through time, his head was pounding.

Tucker slowly sat up and put a hand on his forehead. "Why does it hurt so much?" he asked.

Maya was already on her feet. She stuck the violin into her messenger bag. Then she shrugged. "I don't know," she said. "It doesn't bother me at all." She put out a hand to help Tucker up.

"Besides, we have bigger problems," Maya said. "I think we're in the wrong place . . . or, um, wrong time, or whatever. The boat is fine. Maybe we came back too soon."

Tucker looked around. They seemed to be in a very fancy-looking lounge. It was a beautiful room, with carved wood and luxurious chairs and couches. A few people were standing around, chatting and laughing. Maya was right. Everything did seem fine — other than the pain in Tucker's head.

"Are you okay, lad?" a voice nearby asked.

Tucker and Maya turned. A man in a black suit stood there. He wasn't wearing a tie, and his shirt collar was open. In one hand, he held a small glass. In the other, he held a cigar. He looked at Tucker and Maya with his forehead furrowed in concern.

The man noticed that Tucker's hand was still on his head. "You must have taken a fall," the man said. "That was quite the little bump we had, eh?"

"Um, little bump?" Maya repeated.

"It's nothing to worry about, I'm sure," the man said. "We've stopped for moment, but we should be moving along soon enough."

"What happened?" Tucker asked.

"It's not entirely clear," the man said. "Some minor incident, I'm sure. You needn't worry." With that, he turned and walked back to the group of passengers standing nearby.

"I don't get it," Tucker whispered to Maya. "Maybe we haven't hit the iceberg yet."

Maya shrugged. "Beats me," she said. "Maybe the violin brought us back too early. Should we go back and try the life vest?"

Tucker looked around the lounge. Most of the men were not wearing their ties. Many had taken off their suit jackets. Their sleeves were folded up.

The women were wearing coats, as if they'd been outside, but it was quite warm in the lounge. Something seemed off. It looked like they were standing in one of the first-class lounges. So why was everyone dressed so casually?

"Something isn't right," Tucker said. He looked around the room quickly and spotted a clock. It was almost midnight, not long after they'd left their last trip to the *Titanic*.

Maya was strolling off, looking at the fancy decorations. "I know," she said. "We messed up. I already said we should go back and try again."

"I don't think we messed up," Tucker said. "I think all these people messed up."

"What do you mean?" Maya asked, turning around.

"I mean I think we already hit the iceberg," Tucker said. "Look at the clock. It's almost midnight. *Titanic* hit the iceberg at 11:40 p.m. We're already sinking. But none of these people seem to realize it."

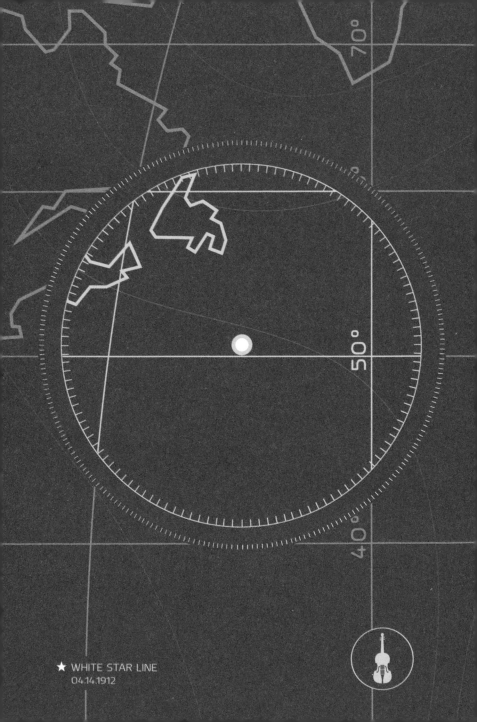

4

BERT TERRELL

"It doesn't seem like these people know they hit an iceberg," Maya said. She looked around at the group of first-class passengers. They were chatting and laughing. Everyone was talking loudly, like they were at some weird party. But no one seemed upset. No one was crying or running for lifeboats. There didn't seem to be a reason to.

"Let's go see what's happening," Tucker said. He grabbed Maya, and they went out on deck.

The scene on the boat deck was eerily similar. Everyone was bundled up in heavy coats. A few crewmen were there, but they didn't seem any more concerned than the first-class passengers.

Tucker recognized Seaman Bert Terrell, the crewman who had helped them find Liam during their last trip through time.

"Bert!" Tucker called out. He raised his arm and waved to get Bert's attention.

Bert turned. His eyes lit up in recognition. Maya and Tucker hurried across the deck toward him. "What are you two doing up here?" Bert asked when they reached him. "Didn't I leave you both down in Miss Jessop's quarters?"

"Um, yeah," Tucker said. "We . . . uh . . . we felt a bump. We wanted to see what was happening."

"And you came all the way up on deck?" Bert asked, frowning. He crossed his arms and looked from Tucker's face to Maya's.

"What?" Tucker said. "Why not?"

Bert leaned down. "The incident was only a few minutes ago," he said quietly. "You couldn't have made it up to the boat deck that quickly. That's impossible."

"Well, uh . . . ," Tucker started to say.

Maya stammered, "We were . . ."

Luckily, neither had to go on, because one of the first-class men tapped Bert on the shoulder.

"Young man," the other man said. "What is happening, exactly?"

A woman nearby stepped up to them too. "Yes," she said. "Is there some kind of trouble?"

"It felt like we hit something a little while ago," another man said. "Did it damage the ship?"

Soon, Bert, Tucker, and Maya were surrounded by a group of curious first-class passengers.

"Please, gentlemen and ladies," Bert said. He put up his hands, palms out, and tried to calm everyone down. "I don't know any more than you do. As soon as my commanding officer gives me any information or instructions, I'll let you know."

Just then, another man in fancy clothes came out onto the deck. "Well, I know what happened," he said loudly. "We've hit an iceberg."

Some of the women gasped and clutched their husbands' arms. The man standing closest to Maya and Tucker chuckled. "An iceberg, was it?" he said. "Felt more like an ice cube to me."

Some of the other men laughed as well.

"It was an iceberg," Tucker insisted. "This is serious!"

The men looked at Tucker silently for a moment. Then they burst into laughter.

"Very serious?" one of them asked. "Are we sinking, lad?"

"Yes!" Tucker and Maya said together.

That made everyone positively hysterical with laughter.

"Son, the *Titanic* won't sink," a woman said. "It's an unsinkable ship."

Bert nodded. "It really is," he said to Tucker. Then he turned to the man with the news about the iceberg. "How do you know that we've hit an iceberg?"

The man held up a drinking glass. "I was sitting near the window in the smoking room," he said. "I saw the thing."

"See?" Tucker said. "It's no joke. The *Titanic* hit an iceberg! Why aren't you all more worried?"

Another of the first-class passengers stepped forward and held up his drink. "My drink has gotten rather warm," he said. "Someone scrape off some of that berg to chill my drink."

Everyone laughed again. Even Bert chuckled and shook his head. No one seemed to think there was any real problem.

"Why doesn't anyone care?" Maya asked Tucker. "Are they all crazy?"

"I don't know," Tucker said. "But if we don't do something soon, no one's going to get on those lifeboats. And that includes Liam."

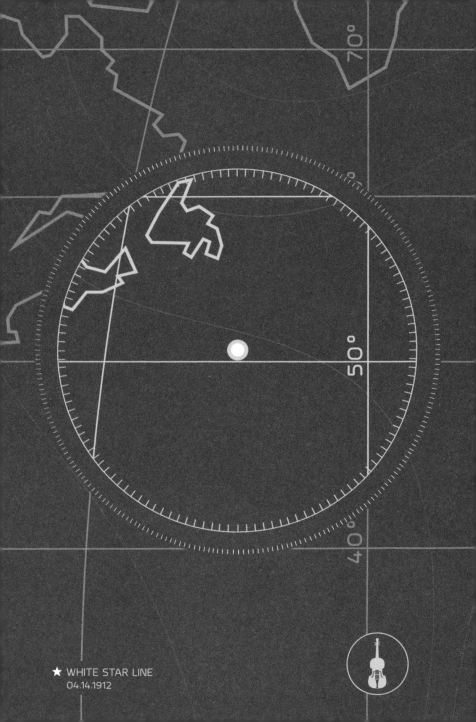

70°

50°

40°

★ WHITE STAR LINE
04.14.1912

THE GYM

"Ladies and gentlemen," a crewman called from inside an open doorway. "Please, come inside from the deck. There is nothing to be concerned about."

"What is going on?" someone asked. "When can we return to our cabins? This is all quite ridiculous. It's freezing out here."

"I believe," said the man in the uniform, "that we've simply turned sharply to avoid the iceberg. There's nothing to worry about. We'll be moving and back on course any moment. Once it's sorted out, you can return to your cabins."

"What?" Maya whispered to Tucker. "That's not what happened at all. They can't believe that!"

Tucker shrugged. "Maybe the crew doesn't want anyone to panic," he said quietly.

"What are we supposed to do in the meantime?" a woman called out.

"That's right," another said. "We're too excited to go back to bed."

"I've opened the gymnasium, no tickets required," the man said. He gestured to a nearby door. "Please, try out some of our equipment."

"At this time of night?" a young woman asked incredulously.

The man with her laughed. He flicked his mustache and put an arm around the young woman. "It'll be a laugh," he said. "Come on, dear." Then he led her through the door and into the gymnasium.

"If it's good enough for Mr. Astor," a man nearby said to a woman at his side, "then I imagine it's good enough for me."

She nodded, and soon everyone on the deck was heading into the gym.

After a few minutes, Tucker and Maya stood alone with Bert again.

"Who was that guy?" Maya asked. "The one with the mustache, I mean — Mr. Astor."

"Don't you know?" Bert asked. "That was John Jacob Astor. He's a famous inventor and writer. He's a millionaire."

Tucker and Maya looked at each other blankly, then back at Bert. They both shrugged.

"He's an American," Bert added. "He's the wealthiest man onboard the ship!"

Tucker and Maya shook their heads. "Sorry, not ringing any bells," Maya said.

"That woman with him was his new young bride, Madeleine," Bert said. He leaned closer to whisper, "She's in a delicate condition. It's been in all the newspapers."

"I think that means she's pregnant," Maya whispered to Tucker.

"Sorry," Tucker said to Bert. "We've never heard of them."

Bert put his fists on his hips. "Unbelievable. Children nowadays," he said. "Well, let's get inside, anyway. You two can get a look at the gym. I don't think anyone will mind if a couple of children pop in under my watch."

* * *

The gym was like nothing Maya or Tucker had ever seen. The equipment didn't look anything like the exercise equipment they were used to. Instead, there was a huge machine that might have been a torture device if not for the oars attached to it. It seemed to be some type of old-fashioned rowing machine. There were also two very odd devices Maya and Tucker couldn't identify.

The wealthy man — Mr. Astor — was sitting on one of the weird machines with his young wife. They'd both put on life vests.

"This doesn't look like a gym," Maya said.
"What's with all the wooden stuff?"

Bert made a confused face. "That's the
equipment, of course," he said. He nodded toward
the wooden equipment the Astors were sitting
on. "That's the electric horse."

"Look here, darling," Mr. Astor said to his
wife. He held a third life vest in his lap. He pulled
a knife from his pocket and stabbed the life vest.

"What are you doing?" Tucker cried. He ran over and tried to snatch the jacket away. "Someone will need that!"

The room went dead silent. Several people gasped.

Mr. Astor stared at Tucker for a moment. Then he threw his head back and laughed. "Oh, I've missed American youth," he said. "So full of . . . vigor."

He reached out and took the life vest back from Tucker. "I think the ship can spare this one jacket, son," Mr. Astor said. "My wife was doubting the ability of these jackets to hold us afloat — not that we'd need them. I thought I'd show her what was inside," he said. "To put her mind at ease."

Mr. Astor turned back to his wife and put a hand on her shoulder. "Not that it will come to that, my dear," he said.

Maya strolled over and tried to sneak a look. "So?" she said. "What is inside?"

"Cork!" Mr. Astor said, holding up the jacket. "See, they'll be plenty buoyant!"

Several of the first-class passengers said, "Ahh!"

Tucker and Maya rolled their eyes. "This guy's a brilliant inventor?" Maya muttered under her breath.

Tucker laughed. "We're wasting our time here," he said. "Let's get down to third class. We have to find Liam. We don't have any time to waste."

Maya nodded. "You're right," she said. "We don't have much time. Even if none of these people realize it, *Titanic* is going to sink. By 2:20 a.m., this is all going to be under water."

Tucker swallowed hard. He didn't want to think about what would happen to all these people — not to mention him and Maya — if they were still onboard at that time.

"Let's go," Tucker said. He turned to Bert. "Bye, Bert. We're going to find Liam."

"Off to have a little adventure with your friend?" Bert asked. "All right. Might as well. All of third class is probably awake after that bump, anyway. Stay out of trouble."

Maya and Tucker nodded and hurried out of the gym. As they walked back onto the boat deck, the ship lurched to one side. With no warning or chance to brace themselves, Maya and Tucker were pitched straight toward the railing and the dark ocean below.

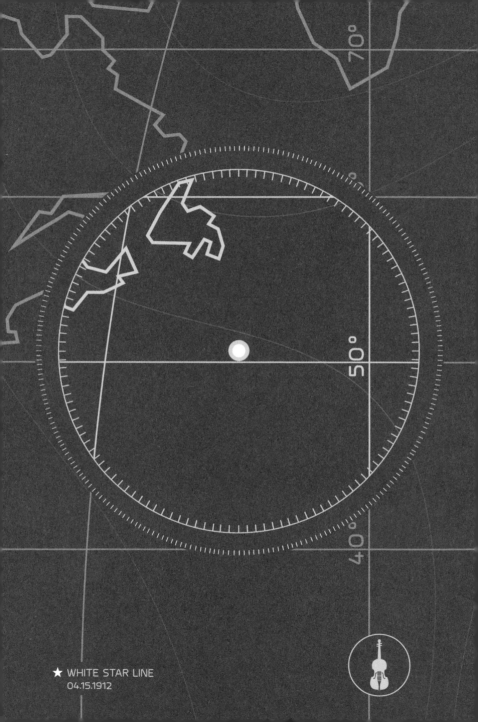

70°

50°

40°

★ WHITE STAR LINE
04.15.1912

6

NOTHING TO WORRY ABOUT

Tucker was rushing toward the railing, unable to stop. As he fell, he could hear Maya beside him, screaming at the top of her lungs. With the ship's deck at an angle, Tucker could see the dark water of the Atlantic Ocean rushing up to meet them.

An instant later, both kids slammed into the iron railing that ran around the outside of the deck.

They stopped suddenly, but Maya's bag, holding the violin, kept going. It slid off her shoulder as she hit the railing. It would have fallen over the railing and into the water below if she hadn't grabbed it at the last minute. Maya yanked the bag back and pressed it close to her body.

"What was that?" Maya shouted.

"I don't know," Tucker said breathlessly. "But it was really scary. We can't risk losing that violin."

"No kidding," Maya said. Her eyes were wide with fear, and she clutched her bag tightly. "Without the violin we're stuck here. And I don't know about you, but I don't want to be anywhere near this ship in a couple of hours."

Bert was behind them in an instant. He put a hand on each of their shoulders. "We've just listed a bit," he said. "I'm sure everything is fine. Are you both okay?"

"Listed?" Tucker repeated in disbelief.

Bert nodded. "Just a little tilt, really," he said. "Nothing to worry about. You two go on and find your friend now."

Tucker and Maya turned and made their way to the door leading to the staircase. As they pulled open the door that lead down to D Deck, Tucker said, "Nothing to worry about? Is he kidding? That was not a little tilt."

"Yeah, you think?" Maya said. She pointed below.

They both looked down. From where they stood at the top of the stairs, Maya and Tucker should have been able to see all the way down to the deck below. But they couldn't. The bottom of the stairs was already covered with water. It filled the hallway below and lapped against the bottom of the stairs as it continued to rise.

"The water is already rising!" Maya shouted.

Tucker nodded. "The front of the ship is already filling with water," he said. "We'd better figure out another way down to third class, quick!"

The kids exited the stairway at B Deck and ran through the narrow halls toward the rear of the ship. As they turned a corner, Tucker spotted another doorway. "I think there's a way down over here!" he called.

Tucker yanked the door open. But as he did, he felt a hand grab his collar and drag him backward. Out of the corner of his eye, he could see Maya next to him. She was being pulled backward, away from the doorway, too.

"And just where do you two think you're going?" a stern voice said.

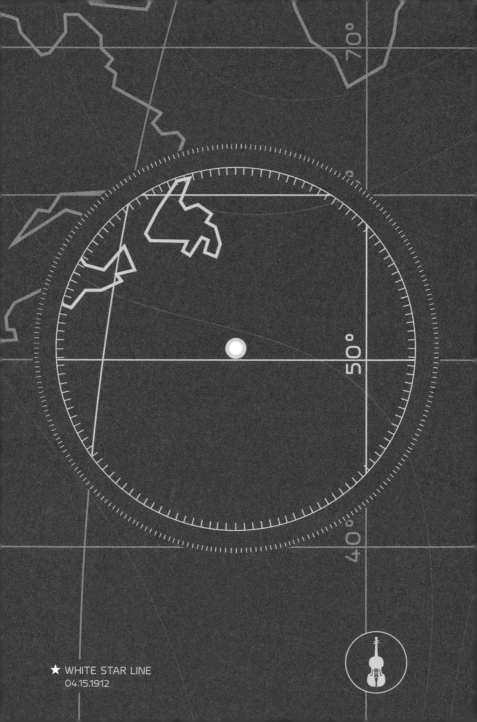

70°

0°

50°

40°

★ WHITE STAR LINE
04.15.1912

7

VIOLET JESSOP

Tucker and Maya twisted and turned, trying to get away.

"Let go of me!" Maya shouted. She tugged with all her strength and freed herself. She tumbled to the floor. Then she jumped to her feet and spun, ready to attack whoever had grabbed her.

It was Violet Jessop, the stewardess whose quarters they were supposed to be sleeping in right now. Her dark auburn hair was pulled back and she looked like she'd gotten dressed in a hurry. Her stewardess outfit was wrinkled, and her hat was slightly crooked.

"I've been looking all over for you two!" Violet snapped. "Do you know how worried I've been? When the collision woke me up, you were both gone!"

Tucker looked at his feet, embarrassed. He hadn't even considered that Violet might be worried.

Maya didn't have the same concerns. She stamped one foot. "We had to sneak out!" she said. "We've been telling everyone for like three days that we were going to hit an iceberg."

"You have?" Violet asked.

"And no one would listen," Maya said. "So now it's too late. We have to find Tucker's friend Liam to help him and his parents get to a lifeboat."

Tucker looked up. "Third-class passengers had trouble getting to the lifeboats," he explained.

Maya rolled her eyes and elbowed Tucker in the side. "They probably *will* have trouble," Maya quickly corrected him. "He meant to say they probably will have trouble."

Violet sighed. "I don't fully understand this," she said. Her Irish accent was more obvious than before. "But I have orders to help get passengers onto lifeboats, and that is exactly what I intend to do — starting with you two."

Tucker and Maya quickly dodged as Violet reached for their collars again.

"Not without Liam and his family," Tucker insisted.

"I am losing my patience with you two," Violet said.

"In that case," Maya said, taking Tucker by the hand, "I apologize in advance for this." She turned to Tucker. "Let's go," she said, and they took off running down the deck.

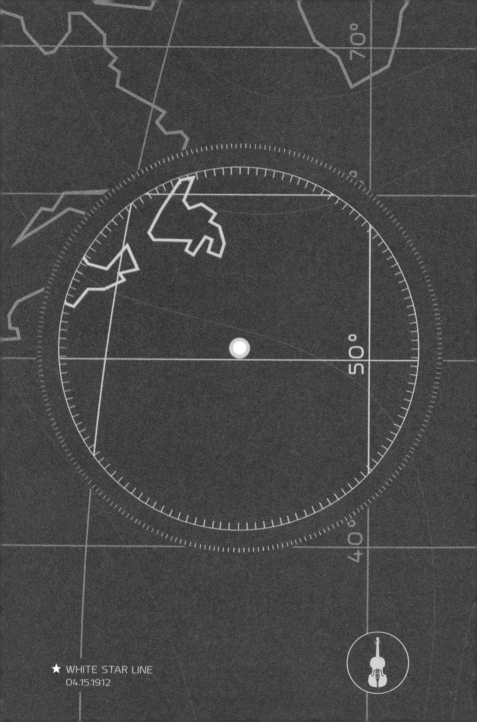

70°

50°

40°

★ WHITE STAR LINE
04.15.1912

8

THIRD CLASS

"Stop!" Violet called after them.

Maya and Tucker ran as fast as they could. The deck was becoming crowded as more passengers and crew began to assemble outside. Crewmembers were urging women and children into the lifeboats on deck.

As they ran, Tucker saw Mr. Astor and his wife, along with several other first-class passengers, back out on the deck. "We'll stay here," Mr. Astor was saying to one of the stewards. "We are safer here than on that little boat."

Tucker and Maya kept running. They dodged between seamen and stewardesses. They ducked around corners and headed for the back stairs. Before long, they'd lost Violet easily.

"This way, I think," Tucker said. He led Maya toward the stairway closest to the rear of the ship. Soon they were in the third-class quarters — or they should have been. Instead, they found a locked gate blocking their way.

On the other side of the gate, dozens of third-class passengers shouted to be let out. Several male passengers rattled the metal gate in frustration.

When they saw Tucker and Maya, a man at the front of the group yelled, "Open the gate, lad!" and "Let us out, lassie!"

Two *Titanic* crewmen stood near the gate on the same side as Tucker and Maya. One seemed quite nervous. He was anxiously trying to calm down the third-class passengers trapped on the other side.

"Please," the crewman said. "Everyone, just remain calm. We can't open the gate without orders from our commanding officer. Please, stop screaming."

The other crewman was less concerned. He leaned on the wall nearby. "Don't bother," he said. "We're not opening that gate until all of the first-class passengers are safe."

Tucker was furious. He stomped over to the crewmen. "Open this gate!" he said.

The crewman rolled his eyes. "Wonderful," he said. "Now they're shouting at us from this side, too."

Maya approached the other crewman. "He's right," she said. "These people are in real danger. You can't keep them trapped down here!"

The crewman scratched his chin. "I doubt there's any real danger, young lady," he said.

Maya sighed. "Not you, too," she said. "I thought down here people would realize we were in trouble."

The other crewman chuckled. "Lass, this ship is unsinkable," he said. "Haven't you heard? There are sixteen watertight compartments below us. If we have a hull breach, the doors between the compartments will seal closed. I assure you, the ship will not sink."

"That's right," the other crewman agreed. "Even if four of the compartments fill with water, we'll have enough buoyancy to stay afloat. There's no cause for alarm."

Just then Violet Jessop appeared. She was out of breath from chasing after Maya and Tucker, but she'd heard what the crewmen were saying. "But what if the water escapes from those compartments?" she said.

The crewman shook his head calmly. "Can't happen, love," he said. "Watertight, like I said."

"It already has happened!" Maya said. "Tucker and I saw the front stairs filling with water."

Violet crossed her arms and looked at them very seriously. "Are you sure?" she asked.

Tucker and Maya nodded.

Violet set her jaw and approached the crewmen. "Open this gate, lads," she said.

The crewman shook his head. "Can't do it, ma'am," he said. "We've got to wait for orders."

"Very well," Violet said. "I'll take care of it myself, then."

She marched over to the gate and pulled out a set of keys. Selecting the right one, she quickly unlocked the gate. As soon as it was unlocked, the third-class passengers on the other side cheered and shoved it open. A wave of people came charging out.

Tucker ran over to Maya. "Do you see Liam anywhere?" he hollered above the noise.

Maya shook her head no. It was impossible to

find anyone in the mass of people rushing for the stairs. There were dozens of children, women, and men. Nearly everyone was carrying something. Those who weren't carrying babies or small children were loaded down with bundles and packages.

"Liam must be here someplace," Maya said.

Tucker tried to peer through the crowd, but he couldn't make out any of the faces. "Let's go up with them," he said. "We'll have better luck finding him up on deck."

As the huge crowd of third-class passengers — now joined by Tucker, Maya, and Violet — reached the last flight of stairs to the boat deck, they all stopped. Several people in the back of the group nearly walked right into the people at the front.

"What's the delay?" someone shouted. "Is there another gate? Let us through!"

"Open it for us, Miss Jessop," someone said. A few people laughed and cheered at that.

Tucker and Maya shoved their way to the front of the crowd. There was no gate. Instead, a group of first-class men and a couple of *Titanic* crewmen stood at the top of the stairs.

"Look at them," one man said. He took a puff of his cigar. "Why are they carrying so much stuff? Do they think we've arrived in New York?"

Several of the men laughed. Most of the third-class passengers kept their mouths shut. These were some of the wealthiest men in the world. Everyone seemed hesitant to stand up to them.

Just then, a small voice carried across the crowd. "We're carrying everything we can! It's everything we own, and we don't want to see it lost in the Atlantic!"

Everyone in the crowd turned to see who'd spoken. It was Liam. He was carrying a heavy-looking sack over one shoulder and had a wool cap pulled down tight on his head. Behind him stood his mother. Her hand rested on Liam's shoulder. She, too, had a bag on her shoulder.

Liam's father dropped his sack and pulled off his cap. He looked up at the men at the top of the steps. "I think you'd better let us through," he said, staring the man who'd spoken in the eyes.

Maya elbowed Tucker. "Your friend Liam," she whispered, "is pretty cool."

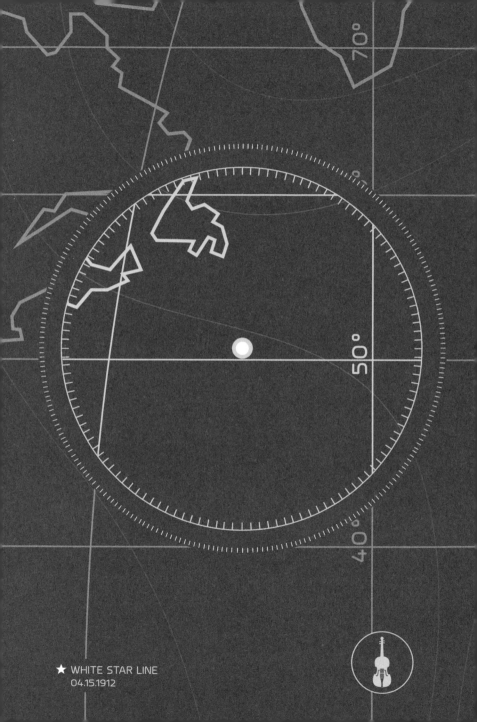

WOMEN AND CHILDREN FIRST

Violet stomped up the last few steps to where the first-class men stood blocking the way. "Please step aside," she said sternly. "There are women and children coming up."

The men at the top of the steps quickly stopped laughing. They averted their eyes and looked ashamed. Without a word, they stepped aside. The group of third-class passengers started up the stairs.

"What was that all about?" Maya whispered to Tucker as they moved past.

Tucker shrugged. When they reached the top of the stairs, Bert was standing there. "Violet's a spirited woman, isn't she?" he said.

Maya and Tucker barely nodded as they looked around. The scene on deck was totally different from the one they'd left. Instead of standing around joking or passing the time, the men were busy helping women and children into lifeboats. It seemed people had finally begun to realize the severity of the situation.

Near the railing, a crewmember shot a distress rocket into the air with a loud bang. A shower of white stars exploded against the night sky several hundred feet above the ship.

Mr. and Mrs. Astor were still on deck. As Tucker and Maya watched, Mr. Astor helped his wife climb into a lifeboat. She looked young and scared. He held his wife's hand as she settled on the hard bench seat.

"May I board with her?" Mr. Astor shouted to the crewman on the lifeboat.

"I'm sorry, sir, but no. Captain's orders, sir," the crewman said. "Women and children first."

Mrs. Astor sobbed and reached for her husband.

"Please, can't you see she's hysterical?" Mr. Astor asked. "Let me board. She's in a delicate condition."

But the crewman waved him away. "Women and children first," he repeated sternly. "Captain's orders."

Mr. Astor nodded sadly. He leaned over and said something to his wife that Maya and Tucker couldn't hear. Then he turned away from the lifeboat.

Behind him were two children. Mr. Astor picked one up by the shoulders and placed her in the lifeboat. Then he walked off toward the first-class lounge.

"Why are only women and children allowed on the lifeboats?" Maya asked.

Bert, who had also been watching Mr. Astor try to board, put a hand on Maya's shoulder. "It's naval tradition, I suppose," he said. "Don't fret about it."

"But wouldn't it be better if that man could be with his wife?" Tucker asked. "You said she's in a 'delicate condition,' right? He should be with his family."

"Now, don't worry," Bert said. "Everyone is going to be just fine. You'll see. I'm sure the lifeboats are just a precaution. Mr. Astor will be reunited with his wife in no time at all."

"How can you say that?" Maya asked incredulously. "There aren't enough lifeboats for everyone on board."

Violet stepped between them. "Don't be a fool, Seaman Terrell," she said. "We've been below. The water is well out of the watertight compartments now."

"It is?" Bert asked. He sounded genuinely surprised.

Violet nodded. "We need to start saving as many people as we can," she said. "And that means getting them off this ship. Now let's get to it."

At Violet's words, Bert's face grew quickly serious. "All right," he said. Even though he couldn't have been out of his teens, Bert suddenly seemed very adult.

Bert and Violet snapped into action. They moved over to a group of third-class passengers and began urging them toward the lifeboats. Tucker and Maya watched as families were divided and prized possessions were left behind.

Liam stood beside them. "Most of these people never planned to return home," he said sadly. He shook his head. "They were starting new lives in America. Everything they have in the world is onboard *Titanic*."

"They were moving?" Maya asked. "To America?"

Liam nodded. "Most of the third-class passengers are moving to America for a better life. That's why we're going."

"Where are your parents?" Tucker asked.

Liam pointed across the deck to where his

father and mother were speaking to Violet. "I imagine they're trying to sort things out with Miss Jessop," he said.

"We have to get you onto a lifeboat," Tucker said. He took Liam by the arm.

Liam pulled away. "Don't bother," he said. "That crewman wasn't joking before. No third-class passengers will be put on a lifeboat before all the first-class women and children are safe."

"That's not fair!" Maya said.

Liam shrugged. "Who said anything about fair?" he said.

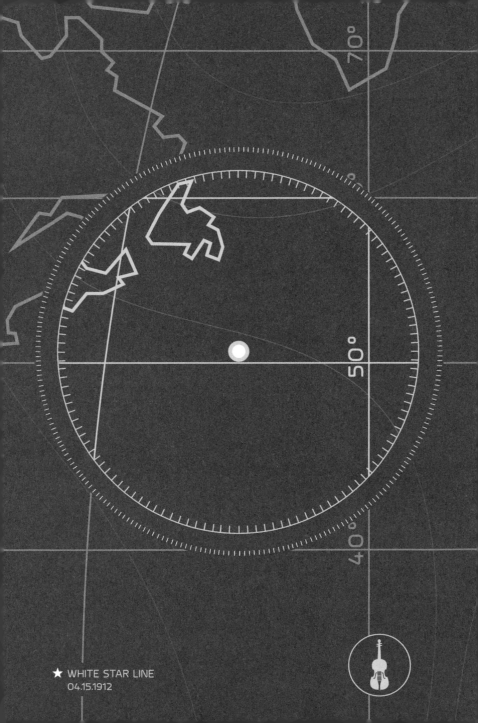

10

THE BAND PLAYS ON

"Come on," Liam said. "We might as well make use of this time. I haven't seen much of first class. Let's have a look around."

"How can you be so calm about this?" Tucker asked. "There's room in these lifeboats! Some of them aren't even half full, and you and your parents still aren't allowed to board. Why aren't you more upset?"

"I'm hardly happy about it," Liam said as he walked across the deck. "But I'm used to it. You wouldn't understand. You're Americans. I've heard things are a little different in your country."

Tucker and Maya glanced at each other. "Very different," Maya muttered, "especially where we come from."

Liam snuck a peek into the first-class lounge. His eyes went wide. "Wow," he said. "Look at this."

The three kids peered into the lounge. People were passing through quickly as they realized how urgent the situation had become. No one seemed concerned with three third-class children being in a first-class area now.

Things sure have changed since our first trip, Tucker thought.

"Look at that," Maya said. "What are they doing?"

Tucker and Liam both looked in the direction Maya was pointing. Across the deck, *Titanic's* small orchestra was sitting down and playing.

"Seems like an odd time for a concert," Liam said.

"They must be crazy," Tucker said.

"Totally insane," Maya said.

"I think it's lovely," said Violet, who had come up behind them. "In fact, I'd say Mr. Hartley and his musicians are real heroes tonight."

"Heroes?" Maya said, spinning around to face Violet. "They're not saving anyone. They're just sitting there. They'll all drown if they don't get to a lifeboat!"

Violet didn't take her eyes off the orchestra.

"Violet?" Maya said. "Hello?" When Violet still didn't respond, Maya turned and watched the orchestra too. After a moment, so did Liam and Tucker.

"What song is it?" Maya asked quietly.

Violet patted a handkerchief against the corners of her eyes. "I think," she said, "it is 'Nearer My God to Thee.'"

The four of them stood listening to the music as frantic passengers rushed around them, trying to find a spot on the rapidly filling lifeboats. It was becoming obvious that there wouldn't be enough space for everyone onboard. And *Titanic* was quickly foundering.

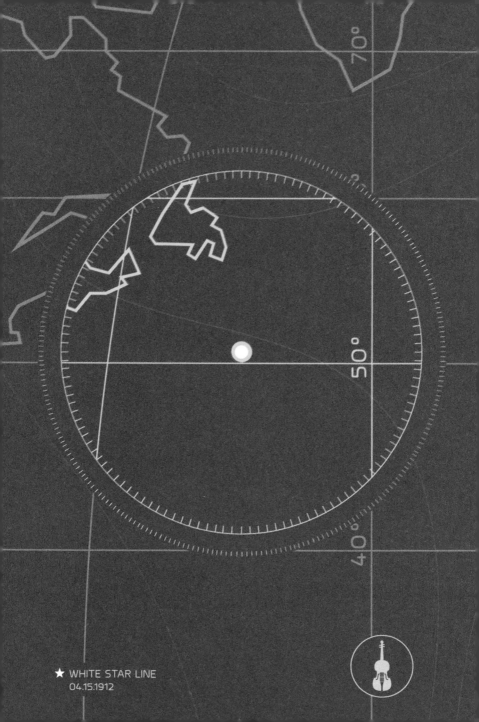

11

LIFEBOATS

"I think it's time for us to board a lifeboat," Violet said. "We cannot wait any longer. Tucker and Maya, the captain made you two my responsibility, so please come with me now." She started to pull them toward one of the lifeboats.

"But what about Liam?" Tucker asked. "What about his parents?"

Violet got down on one knee in front of Liam. "Where are your parents, child?" she asked.

Liam gestured toward the door that led back out on deck. "Speaking with Seaman Terrell, I think, miss," he said.

Violet stood up. "Let's go find them quickly, then," she said.

The four of them walked across the deck to where Mr. and Mrs. Kearney stood, talking to Bert.

Just then, the ship listed heavily toward the bow. People screamed as they — and their belongings — slid across the deck. Tucker heard a splash as something hit the water.

"Don't panic!" a crewman shouted. He was already in lifeboat fourteen, which had just started descending toward the Atlantic.

"Let us on!" a man yelled angrily. He was standing in a small group of men near the railing. "There's room on these lifeboats." He backed up, as if getting ready to leap into the lowering lifeboat.

"Women and children only!" the crewman said. "Now back up! You'll capsize us if you jump!" He waved something in front of him, and a few people gasped.

Tucker and Maya ran forward to get a better look.

"He won't use it," someone said, and the crowd of men — Tucker thought they were from third class — rushed forward.

Violet shrieked so loudly she could be heard over the screaming. "Children!" she yelled. "Step back from there . . . now!"

The air suddenly cracked. Two bright flashes exploded in the darkness. A woman screamed. There was another crack, followed by another flash of light.

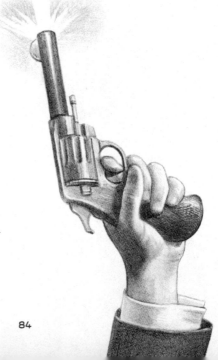

Maya grabbed Tucker's hand, and they pressed against Violet.

"A gun," Tucker whispered. "He has a gun."

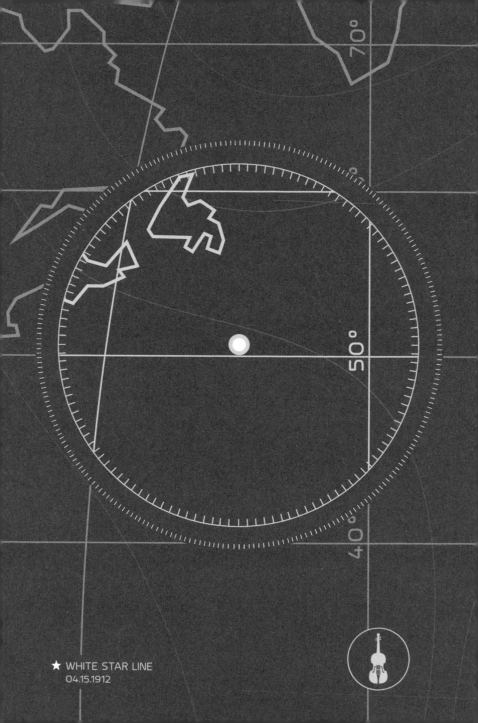

★ WHITE STAR LINE
04.15.1912

12

SHOTS FIRED!

Violet grabbed Maya and Tucker and pulled them down. They fell to their knees beside her.

People screamed. Women and children ran across the deck. Some were crying.

"Please, stay calm!" someone shouted. It was Bert. He stepped right into the fray. "No one has been hurt," he added quickly.

Just then, Captain Smith himself appeared. "What's happening here?" he asked.

"I'm sorry, Captain," Bert said. "One of the officers, Officer Lowe I believe, fired shots between *Titanic* and lifeboat fourteen."

"We can't have a riot," Captain Smith said.

"It's what he was trying to avoid," Bert said. "The men would have tried to board the lifeboat while it was being lowered. The women and children onboard already would have been hurt."

The captain seemed to consider this a moment. "No one was hurt?" he asked.

"Not that I know of, Captain," Bert replied.

"It's a matter for another time, then," the captain said. Then he began to walk off.

Maya grabbed the cuff of his coat. "Captain?" she said. "Sir?"

The captain stopped and looked down at Maya, Tucker, and Violet. "You three had better get a few seats on the next lifeboat," the captain said. "Lifeboat sixteen is about to be lowered."

"We will, Captain," Violet said. "Let's go, you two."

"Just a second," Maya said. She was obviously angry and had tears in her eyes. "We warned you, you know."

"Yes," the captain said. "I know. You were those American children screaming about icebergs."

"Yes," Maya said. "We were. You should have listened to us."

Captain Smith sighed and knelt down so he was eye to eye with Maya. "Yes, I should have," he admitted. "You weren't the only ones to warn us. I've got a stack of warnings that came over the wireless overnight."

"Why did you ignore them?" Tucker asked.

"We didn't ignore them," the captain said. "Only one of them ever made it to the bridge. The wireless officer was bogged down with passengers' personal messages. Why, not long ago, we wouldn't have even had that wireless onboard. We've always managed without it in the past."

"You didn't have a backup?" Maya demanded.

"We had a couple of men up in the crow's nest," the captain said. "That's the perch, way up there." He pointed up into the darkness. Tucker and Maya could just make out a speck of light.

"We thought we'd be able to steer around any bergs that appeared," the captain went on. "We thought we'd see them in time. But the sea is too calm — there were no waves breaking against the iceberg. The lookouts couldn't see it until it was too late. We . . . we were wrong."

The captain stood up. "This was my last voyage," he said quietly, looking out to where the lifeboats were carrying passengers away from the foundering ocean liner. "She was supposed to be unsinkable, you know."

The captain seemed to shake himself out of a fog. He turned to Violet. "Get these kids to a lifeboat, miss," he said in a hard voice.

"Aye, sir," Violet replied.

The captain took a deep breath and walked off.

"Where do you think he's going?" Tucker asked quietly.

"To the bridge, I expect," Violet said. "A captain ought to go down with his ship, they say."

"More naval traditions?" Maya asked.

Violet nodded. "Let's get you two to safety," she said.

"But what about Liam?" Tucker asked. They looked around, but they'd somehow lost sight of him. Desperate passengers rushed everywhere. In the fracas, it was impossible to find Liam or his parents.

"I'm sure he'll be fine," Violet said, "but we can't find him now. Let's go."

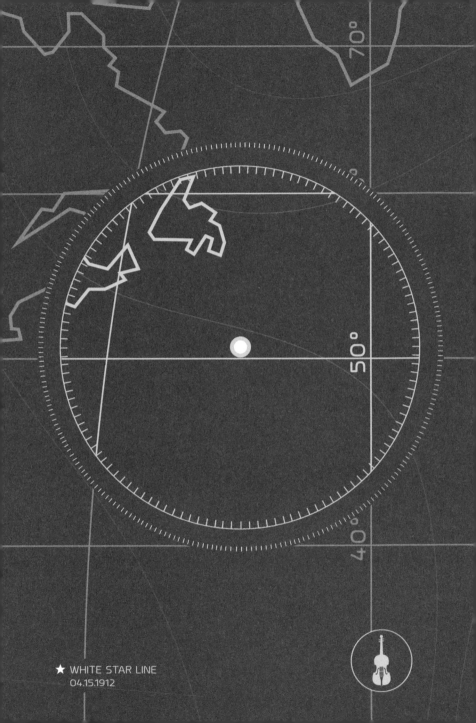

FAILED AGAIN

13

Tucker and Maya squeezed onto the tiny bench seat of lifeboat sixteen. Violet followed them. She was last person allowed to board.

"Hold on," the crewman onboard said. There was a great jerk, and a loud clank as the boat began to drop, slowly, toward the waters of the Atlantic Ocean below.

"Miss Jessop," an officer called from *Titanic*'s deck. "Look after this baby."

Violet glanced up in surprise as the officer dropped a bundle in her lap. Then he disappeared into the growing chaos. Violet held tightly to the bundle as it began to squirm, and finally to scream.

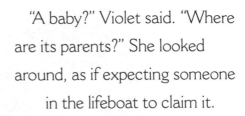

"A baby?" Violet said. "Where are its parents?" She looked around, as if expecting someone in the lifeboat to claim it. Maya and Tucker were no longer listening. They huddled close together on the hard, wooden seat of the lifeboat. At the bottom of the boat, blankets and flares rested near their feet. And pair of long wooden oars stretched over the edges of the lifeboat. The 30-foot boat felt incredibly tiny after the enormity of the *Titanic*.

"We failed," Tucker said. He looked at the bright lights of the *Titanic*, somehow still lit. The bow of the massive ship was slipping slowly under the water. "Liam isn't on a lifeboat."

"You don't know that," Maya said. "He might be. Jeez, I don't think I'd even know if he was on *this* lifeboat."

Tucker shook his head. "If we hadn't been with Violet," he said, "we wouldn't even be on this boat."

Violet looked out over the water. "It's so still," she said. "Why, it's more like a giant pond, isn't it?"

"It's much colder than that, miss," the crewman onboard said.

Suddenly the little boat jerked hard to one side. Tucker slipped from the bench seat and tumbled toward the side of the lifeboat.

In an instant, he was hanging on to the edge of the boat. "Help!" he cried out.

The crewman grabbed his wrists. "Hold on, lad," he said.

But it was no use. In the cold, wet air, neither Tucker nor the crewman could hold on. Tucker slipped. Seconds later, Maya heard the splash as he struck the ocean.

"I have to go, Violet," Maya said. "We'll see you again, soon, though. Like, really soon, I bet."

"Go?" Violet asked. She clutched the baby to her chest. "But your friend . . ."

"I can save him," Maya said. She pulled the violin out of her bag. "But we'll be back. I promise."

Maya took a deep breath. She looked down toward the water. The lifeboat was steady again, and she could just see Tucker struggling against the ice-cold ocean.

"Here we go, Tucker," Maya whispered. Then she dove.

As she fell, Maya tossed the violin as hard as she could. It smashed into the side of the *Titanic*. What was a broken violin splintered even further, into shards and fragments of wood.

Maya never even struck the water.

NEW YORK

GREENVILLE

14

DRY LAND

Tucker woke up coughing water. He was face down on the floor of the storeroom, and he was soaking wet. His head, of course, was pounding. He rolled onto his back.

Maya was standing over him, digging through her messenger bag. "You so owe me," she said. "As usual."

"Um," Tucker said, "thanks. What happened?"

"Well, I saved your life," Maya said. "You fell in the ocean. You would have drowned or froze to death or something. So I had the bright idea of destroying the violin."

"You what?" Tucker said. He sat up. "But someone must have seen! Violet must have noticed when you vanished into thin air."

"Don't worry," Maya said. "I jumped first. No one saw me vanish. No one saw the violin smash."

"Are you sure?" Tucker asked, standing up.

"Positive," Maya said. She peeked into the Special Collection crate and found the violin, once again in its hard plastic case. She sealed up the crate and walked back over to the vent leading back to the conference room.

Tucker followed her to the open vent. He climbed through first, and then waited as Maya crawled through, reattaching the vent covers behind her.

"I'm exhausted," Tucker said once they were back in the conference room. He collapsed into a chair at the long table.

"In that case," Maya said, sitting in the seat next to him, "you'd better finish that homework so you can get a good night's sleep tonight."

"Why?" Tucker asked.

"Because," Maya said, "we have to go back. Tomorrow."

Tucker lifted his head. "I thought you weren't worried about Liam," he said.

"Yeah, well, that was before *Titanic* was actually sinking," Maya said. "We can't just leave him now. What's one more trip? Besides, I think I left my phone on the lifeboat."

CONTINUES IN BOOK

1   2   3   4   ·

OVERBOARD

RETURN TO TITANIC

TIME VOYAGE

1

by STEVE BREZENOFF

①

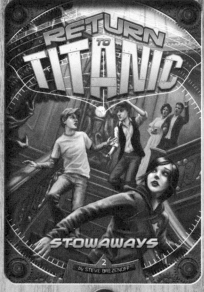

RETURN TO TITANIC

STOWAWAYS

2

by STEVE BREZENOFF

②

RETURN TO TITANIC

AN UNSINKABLE SHIP

3

by STEVE BREZENOFF

③

RETURN TO TITANIC

OVERBOARD

4

by STEVE BREZENOFF

④

PASSENGER MANIFEST

While Tucker, Maya, and Liam are all fictional characters, the story of the *RMS Titanic* and its passengers is very real. In fact, some characters throughout the "Return to Titanic" series are based on real people.

1		**JOHN COFFEY** FIREMAN
2		**VIOLET JESSOP** STEWARDESS
3		**JOHN JACOB ASTOR IV** FIRST-CLASS PASSENGER
4		**EDWARD SMITH** CAPTAIN

J. J. Astor

JOHN JACOB ASTOR IV

John Jacob Astor IV, a character featured in *An Unsinkable Ship*, was a real passenger aboard the *Titanic* when it set sail on its maiden voyage. Astor was a member of the famous Astor family, as well as an American businessman, real estate builder, investor, inventor, and writer.

While traveling abroad, Astor's new wife, Madeleine, discovered she was pregnant. The Astors wanted their child to be born in the United States, so they boarded *Titanic* for her maiden voyage to New York. They were the richest passengers aboard the *Titanic* when it set sail.

Sadly, John Jacob Astor IV did not survive the sinking. He was last seen standing on deck as the lifeboats were lowered. Madeleine Astor later gave birth to their son, John Jacob Astor VI.

HISTORICAL FILES

One of the most interesting stories surrounding the tragic sinking involves *Titanic*'s orchestra, which continued to play even as the great ocean liner sank.

Newpaper Illustration
Richmond Times-Dispatch
April 28, 1912

Titanic Band Members
The Illustrated London News
April 27, 1912

Sheet music aboard *Titanic*
circa 1912

There were actually two separate bands that performed at different times aboard the *Titanic*. The night of the sinking was the first time they would have played together.

Shortly after midnight, bandleader Wallace Hartley assembled the band in the first-class lounge, where many first-class passengers were gathered. The band began to play lively tunes in an effort to keep passengers calm. As more passengers began to realize how serious the situation was and moved to the boat deck, *Titanic*'s band moved as well, near the entrance to the Grand Staircase.

As the tilt of *Titanic*'s deck grew steeper, Hartley released the other musicians and wished them luck. But even as *Titanic*'s stern began to rise out of the water, the band stuck together. Wallace began to play a simple hymn, and the rest of the musicians joined in. It was the last song they would ever play.

Some survivors claim the band's final song was "Nearer, My God, To Thee," while others argue it was "Song d'Automne." Sadly, there can never be a definitive answer, as none of the musicians survived the sinking. One thing that is never debated, however, is that Wallace Hartley and the rest of *Titanic*'s band continued playing bravely until the very end.

Almost two weeks after the disaster, Wallace Hartley's body was recovered from the Atlantic. He was reportedly still wearing his orchestra uniform and had his music box strapped to his chest.

AUTHOR

Steve Brezenoff lives in St. Paul, Minnesota, with his wife, Beth, their son, Sam, and their small, smelly dog, Harry. Besides writing books, he enjoys playing video games, riding his bicycle, and helping middle-school students to improve their writing skills. Steve's ideas almost always come to him in his dreams, so he does his best writing in his pajamas.

ILLUSTRATOR

At a young age, Scott Murphy filled countless sketchbooks with video game and comic book characters. After being convinced by his high school art teacher that he could make a living creating what he loves, Scott jumped headfirst into the artistic pool and hasn't come up for air since. He currently resides in New York City and loves every minute of it.

NEW YORK

★ WHITE STAR LINE
04.2012